Whales

UNIT 18

Illustrated by Robin Koontz

What Is a Whale?

By Richard Dunn
Adapted by Barb Gunn and Jessica Sprick

Cass the Big Blue Whale

By Richard Dunn
Adapted by Barb Gunn and Jessica Sprick

Is It a Whale?

By Jessica Sprick

Vocabulary Words

whale

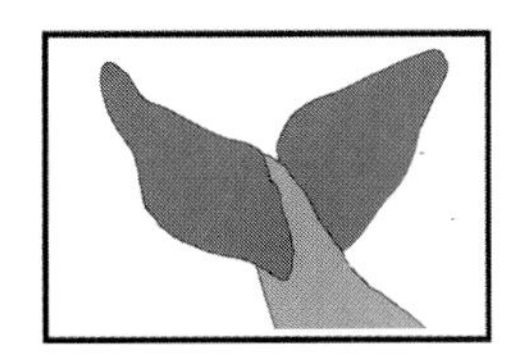

tail fin

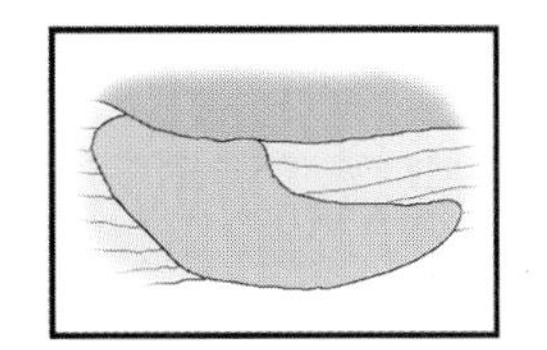

flipper

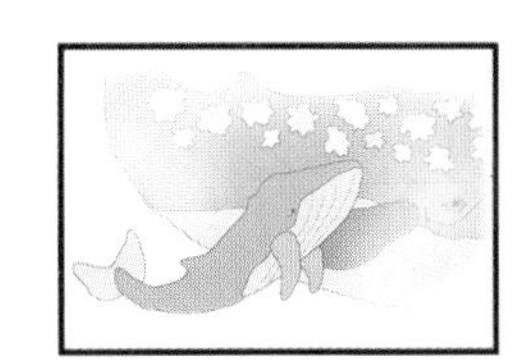

calf

Table of Contents

What Is a Whale?

Cass the Big Blue Whale

Is It a ?

DUET STORIES: Adults read the small text. Students read the large text.

What Is a Whale?

CHAPTER 1 • WHALES ARE MAMMALS

Whales are huge and fascinating animals that live in the sea. Whales look like fish, but whales are really mammals, just like cows, horses, dogs, and people.

Whales are mammals. What other animals are mammals?

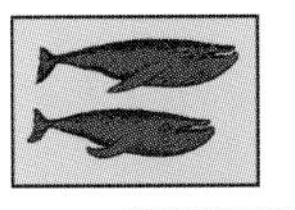 swim in the sea.

A  has flippers to help it steer and keep its balance.

A 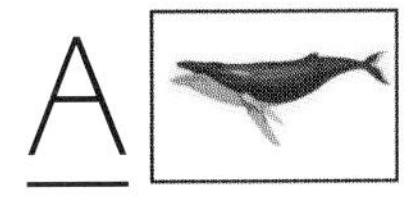 has huge tail fins called flukes that move it through the water.

Look at the picture of the whale. Point to its flipper. Point to its tail fins.

Whales can't breathe under water. So . . .

swim to the surface.

That means that need air.

Whales need air just like people. Whales and people are both . . . mammals.

A whale breathes through holes on the top of its head. The holes are called blowholes. When a whale comes to the surface of the water, it blows water out through its blowhole.
Then the whale breathes in fresh air.

Soon the swims into the dark sea.

Once underwater, whales can hold their breath for long periods of time. One kind of whale can swim underwater for up to 75 minutes without taking a new breath of air.

That's a long time. It's as long as a movie!

A [whale] has a very large brain.

That means a  is a smart mammal.

How do we know a whale is smart? (It has a very large brain.)

 can't see very well, but . . .

 can hear very well.

They hear sounds in the water that help them find their way.

What helps whales find their way? (Sounds in the water)

CHAPTER 2

A Smart 

What is the story about? (A smart whale)

I wish I could see a
swim in the sea.
It would swish and swoosh.

What does the boy want to see? (A whale)

Whack! It would hit the sea with
a hard, hard smack.

Soon the [whale] would swim into the dark, dark sea. Hmmm . . . did that smart [whale] wink at me?

Show me a wink. Do you think a whale would wink at someone?

CHAPTER 3

Whales in the Sea

Whales come in all shapes and sizes. Some whales are enormous.

That means they are very, very big.

The blue whale is the biggest of all the whales. It can grow up to be 100 feet long.

That means it is as long as three school buses put together!

Is a blue whale bigger than one bus? (Yes)

Is a blue whale bigger than two buses? (Yes)

A blue whale is as big as three buses.

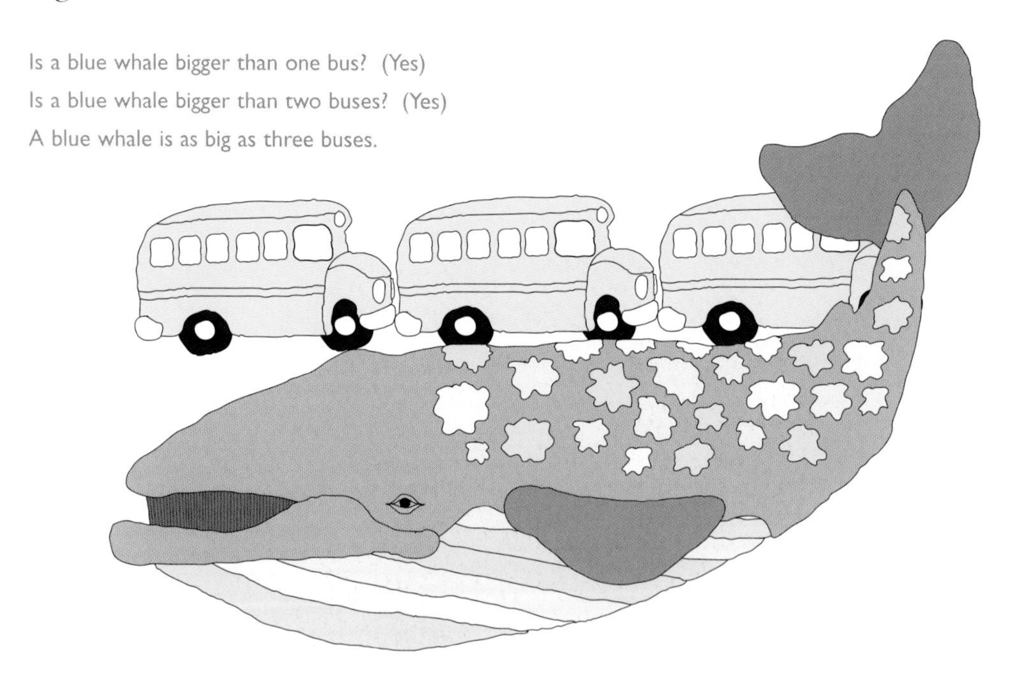

I think that  is enormous!

What does that mean? (A blue whale is very, very big.)

The humpback is a whale with very long flippers. It doesn't really have a hump on its back, but its head and flippers are covered with wart-like lumps.

What can that  do with

its long flippers?

I think it can swoosh and swim in the sea.

Look at the picture of the humpback. Can you see the lumps on its body?

The beluga is a small whale that lives in the cold arctic north. It's only about 10-15 feet in length. That is as long as three to four children lying head to toe.

See the thick ice.

There is a beluga swimming under the ice.

That  needs a hole in the ice so it can come up for air!

Belugas are called white whales because their smooth bodies are the color of milk. I wonder if that makes them look like the ice.

Big or small, lumpy or smooth, all whales begin life as babies, just like people. A baby whale is called a calf.

What's a baby whale called? (A calf)

As soon as a  is born, it swims to the surface with its mother to get air.

The  needs to eat and eat.

It drinks its mother's milk and grows very fast.

See the baby whales. Touch the smallest whale. That calf is one week old. Touch the next calf. It's two weeks old. Touch the bottom whale. That calf is three weeks old. Do whales grow quickly? (Yes)

A blue whale calf gains up to 200 pounds a day!

CHAPTER 4

What Can I Eat?

What's the title of the story? (What Can I Eat?)

"What can I eat?" said the  .
"I swim hard in the sea.
That means I need to eat soon."

Look at the picture. What do you think the whale wants to eat?

The 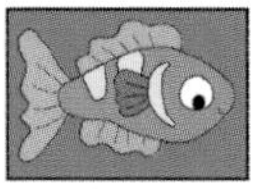 said, "I'm too smart.
That  can't see me in the
weeds."

What's the fish doing? (Hiding in the weeds)

The  couldn't see the 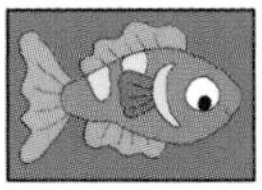 as
it hid in the weeds.

Did the whale get to eat the fish? (No)

Cass the Big Blue Whale

UNIT 18

Main Characters

Mark

Who is this? (Mark)

Ann

Who is this? (Ann)

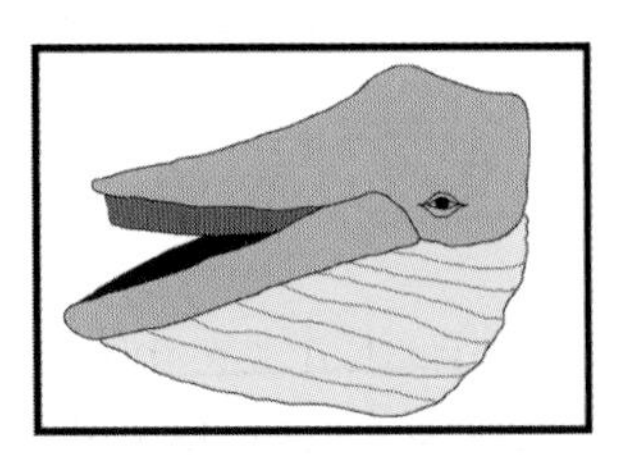

Cass

Who is this? (Cass)

Cass the Big Blue Whale

Ann and Mark were whale researchers. Every day they went out to sea in their boat to study whales.

Ann and Mark had seen beluga whales.

Ann and Mark had seen humpback whales.

But . . .

Mark was sad.

He hadn't seen a

blue whale.

What had Ann and Mark seen?
(Beluga whales, humpback whales)

"I wish we could see a blue whale someday,"

said Mark.

Ann told Mark about a blue whale that she had seen years ago. It was a magnificent whale with a huge scar on its tail. Ann had named the whale Cass.

What had Ann seen? (A blue whale) What did she call the whale? (Cass)

Ann said, "I think Cass isn't around here anymore."

Mark said, "It is dark.

We should go back to shore. Perhaps we'll spot a blue whale tomorrow."
Just then, an enormous tail appeared alongside their boat.

Smack! Whack!

That tail hit the water.
Mark yelled, "Ann, did you see that tail? Did you see that scar?"

"It's Cass!" said Ann. "She has

that scar."

Just then Cass came up for air again. A blue whale calf swam beside her.
Ann said, "Cass has a baby!

That means Cass is a mother now.

Cass and her calf make a magnificent pair!"

Let's give the calf a name. What do you think we should call it?

It had been quite a day. Ann and Mark hadn't seen one great blue whale, they'd seen two — Cass and her new baby.

Is It a ?

What can I see?
What can I see?
Is it a that swims in the sea?

I think I see a
in the sea, sea, sea.
It isn't in a sack,
in a shack, in a tree!

I think I see a .
It isn't a cat.
It isn't a deer,
a , a rat.

Is it a [whale]
that I see, that I see?
It is! It is!
It's a [whale]
in the sea!

UNIT 1
*I
I

UNIT 2
2
see

UNIT 3
me
I'm

UNIT 4
am
Sam

UNIT 5
3
sad
Dad
*said

UNIT 6
Dee
*the
mad

UNIT 7
and
man
seem

UNIT 8
Tamee
meet
that
sat
seems

UNIT 9
we
need
seeds
sweet
Nan
at
weeds
*was
weed

UNIT 10
Tim
sit
in
Matt
sees
Tam
did

UNIT 11
this
*is
Dan
he
*his
Ann
Nat
needs
it
had
an

UNIT 12
cat
can
*has
meets
scat
*wasn't
*a
cats
hit

UNIT 13
ran
trees
*want
can't
win
rat
deer
three
tee hee
near
tree
didn't

UNIT 14
*would
*could
sea
sand
eat
treats
hear
*as
treat

UNIT 14 CONTINUED
Dean
*with
swam
she
swim
wish
seen
*isn't
*should
neat

UNIT 15
think
hid
smack
seat
*couldn't
trick
it's
eats
snack
wink
*he's

UNIT 16
woo
*to
moon
too
dear
noon
dish
moo

UNIT 17
Mark
soon
dark
*are
*do
hard
stars
miss
artist
Sid
thanks
rats
mean
dash
*work

UNIT 18
means
swims
*into
smart
swish
swoosh
whack
*what
thick
Cass
hadn't
scar
sack
shack